a.k.a. The ~~Be~~ ~~B~~ok EVER!

100% offishal

The WHO'S WHONICORN of UNICORNS

Wow!

Original idea
by
Daisy Butters
and
Gabriella Summers

← (They helped a bit) ↘

Kes Gray

Garry Parsons

PUFFIN

IN THE BEGINNING

there was only one single unicorn in the whole wide universe.

He was called **NEWnicorn**
because he was very new.
He was also very lonely.

So **TWOnicorns** were invented too.
TWOnicorns went everywhere in twos . . .

until **FEWnicorns** were invented as well.

Before long there were unicorns everywhere –
unicorns of all shapes and sizes!

Baby unicorns were called . . .
GAGAGOOnicorns.

BLUEnicorns were blue.

MAROONicorns were maroon.

ANYCOLOURYOULIKEIT'SUPTOYOUnicorns

were any colour or colours they wanted to be.

All unicorns loved
having their hair done.

The ones that did the
hair-washing were called
SHAMPOOnicorns.

The ones who did the hair-cutting
were called **HAIRDOnicorns.**

CANOEnicorns lived on the river. They went everywhere by canoe.

Living on the river was really good fun
unless there was a **HARPOONicorn**
hiding in the reeds, trying to get you.

BALLOONicorns had to watch out for **HARPOONicorns** too.

LOOnicorns lived down the loo.

Smelly **LOOnicorns** were called **POOnicorns.**

The really smelly ones were called
STINKYPOOnicorns.

Most unicorns weren't smelly at all.

The scariest unicorns were called **BOO!**nicorns.

BOO!nicorns hid behind trees and jumped out on other unicorns all the time.

MOONicorns only came out at night.

FULLMOONicorns only came out when there was a full moon.

The clumsiest unicorns were called **BUMPINTOnicorns.**
BUMPINTOnicorns bumped into things everywhere they went.

They were always covered in plasters and bruises.

CUCKOOnicorns lived in clocks
and went **"cuckoo!"** all day and night.

LOOPYLOOnicorns had
a horn on their bottom
instead of their head!

Invisible unicorns were called **SEETHROUGHnicorns.**
Sometimes **SEETHROUGHnicorns** would creep up on
BOO!nicorns and make them jump too.

The happiest unicorns were called **YAHOOnicorns.**

The unhappiest were called **BOOHOOnicorns.**

Their best friends were called **TISSUEnicorns.**

The best unicorn fighters were called **KUNGFUnicorns.**
KUNGFUnicorns were black belts in everything!

PUNYcorns were really weedy.

GLUEnicorns stuck together.

SUPERGLUEnicorns
REALLY stuck together!

Unicorns who ate really hot curry were called **VINDALOOnicorns.**

Unicorns who preferred stew were called **STEWnicorns.**
Unicorns who liked cheese were called **FONDUEnicorns.**

HOWDOYOUDOnicorns

were very polite.

THANKYOUnicorns

were very grateful.

AFTERYOUnicorns

had really good manners.

NO,AFTERYOUnicorns

had even better manners.

QUEUEnicorns loved standing in long lines.

SNOOKERCUEnicorns were really good at playing snooker.

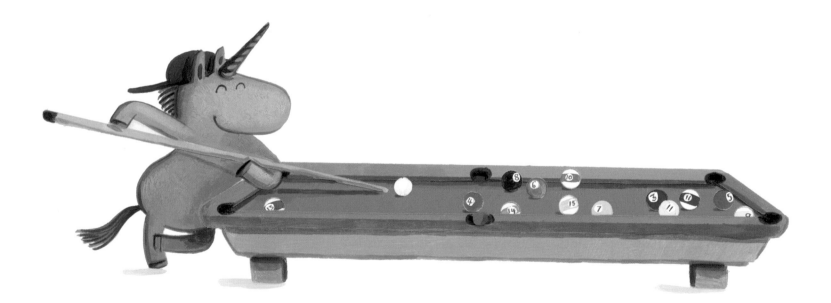

POOLCUEnicorns were really good at playing pool.

NOTHINGTODOnicorns got bored really easily.

HULLABALLOOnicorns

were really noisy.

Unicorns who lived on the top of really high mountains were called
LOOKATTHATVIEW!nicorns.

GREWnicorns never stopped growing.

They just **GREW**

and **GREW**

and **GREW** until . . .

(They exploded!)

THE END

(unless you can think of some more!)

To Daisy Butters & Gabriella Summers,
who gave us the ideas for this book! – K.G. & G.P.

PUFFIN BOOKS is part of the Penguin Random House group of companies
whose addresses can be found at global.penguinrandomhouse.com.
First published 2021
Text copyright © Kes Gray, 2021
Illustrations copyright © Garry Parsons, 2021
The moral right of the author and illustrator has been asserted
Made and printed in Italy   001

The authorized representative in the EEA is Penguin Random House Ireland,
Morrison Chambers, 32 Nassau Street, Dublin D02 YH68

A CIP catalogue record for this book is available from the British Library
ISBN: 978–0–241–52800–6
All correspondence to: Puffin Books, Penguin Random House Children's,
One Embassy Gardens, 8 Viaduct Gardens, London SW11 7BW